This **Lollipop** and *Grandpa* Book

Belongs to:

. . . .

For Mum and Dad who gave me my love of books,
and Grandpa for my love of mischief. PH

For Rog and Reg and EDM. CJ

Lollipop and Grandpa's Back Garden Safari

ISBN: 978-1-907-91209-2

Published in Great Britain by Phoenix Yard Books Ltd

This edition published 2012

Phoenix Yard Books
Phoenix Yard
65 King's Cross Road
London
WC1X 9LW

1 3 5 7 9 10 8 6 4 2

Book design by Insight Design Concepts

Printed in Singapore

A CIP catalogue record for this book is available from
the British Library

www.phoenixyardbooks.com

Lollipop
and
Grandpa's
Back Garden Safari

Penelope Harper
Illustrated by Cate James

Lollipop and Grandpa are going on safari.
They pack their binoculars,
they pack their map.
And they pack some ham sandwiches, because
going on safari can be hungry work.

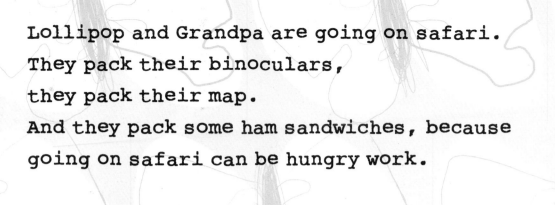

Grandpa leads the expedition.
"Ready, Lollipop?" he cries.
Grandpa loves the wild, and
is pretty wild himself.

"Ready, Grandpa," says Lollipop, who is no stranger to adventure.

They fling open the back door, and suddenly they are plunged deep into the tall grass.

Lollipop and Grandpa must keep their wits about them, because you never know what you'll meet on a back garden safari.

"**Look out, Lollipop!**" says Grandpa.
"You'll be in trouble if he catches
you in his big jaws."

"He will chew you up into tiny little pieces, and
I will have to take you home in a jar and try to put
you back together again."

"Crumbs!" says Lollipop.
"We had better tiptoe past then."
Sssh!
Phew!

Lollipop and Grandpa make it past the
CROCO-LOGUS in **one** piece.
They aren't out of danger yet though,
for out of the bushes lollops a heavy ...

"Look out, Lollipop!"
says Grandpa.

"You'll be in trouble if he sits
on you. He'll squish you so flat
I will have to roll you up like a
carpet, and carry you home over
my shoulder."

"Crumbs!" says Lollipop.
"We had better tiptoe past then."
Sssh!
Phew!

But what's this?
They almost step
straight onto a
sliiiiiippery...

"Look out, Lollipop!"
says Grandpa.

"You'll be in trouble if he takes a
liking to you. He will wrap himself
around you, so I can only see
your head and feet.
Then he will Squeeeeze
you so tight that I will have
to post you home to Mum."

please find
enclosed
one lollipop

"Yikes!" says Lollipop.
"We had better tiptoe past then."
Sssh!
Phew!

Suddenly there's a great whooping and a howling
and a shrieking, and it's coming from high up.
Lollipop takes out her binoculars and sees the...

...CHIMPAN-TREES!

They're leaping and swooping above Lollipop and
Grandpa, their long arms and legs reaching down
towards the intrepid explorers.

"Look out, Lollipop!" says Grandpa.

"You'll be in trouble if they lean down with their long arms and scoop you up. They will tickle and tickle, and tickle and tickle you some more, until you're rolling around on the ground and can't stop laughing. I will have to put you in a box and take you home to Mum."

By this time Lollipop and Grandpa are
feeling hungry, so they decide to get
out their ham sandwich picnic.
They haven't taken more than a couple
of bites when Grandpa freezes.

"Look out, Lollipop!" he says.
"Look over there!"

Lollipop turns and makes a
gasping sound followed by a gulp.

It's the King of the Jungle
himself- the ferocious, the
fearless and the very
hungry looking...

...CLOTHES-LION!

Grandpa whispers to Lollipop. "You'll be in trouble
if he pounces on you. He will..."
But Lollipop has frozen to the spot and isn't listening.

At that moment the Clothes-lion's head spins round to see them,
and then he lets out the most almighty ...

It almost blows Lollipop right off her feet, and it more than ruffles Grandpa's nose hair.

"RUN FOR IT, LOLLIPOP!"

yells Grandpa, already halfway up the path.

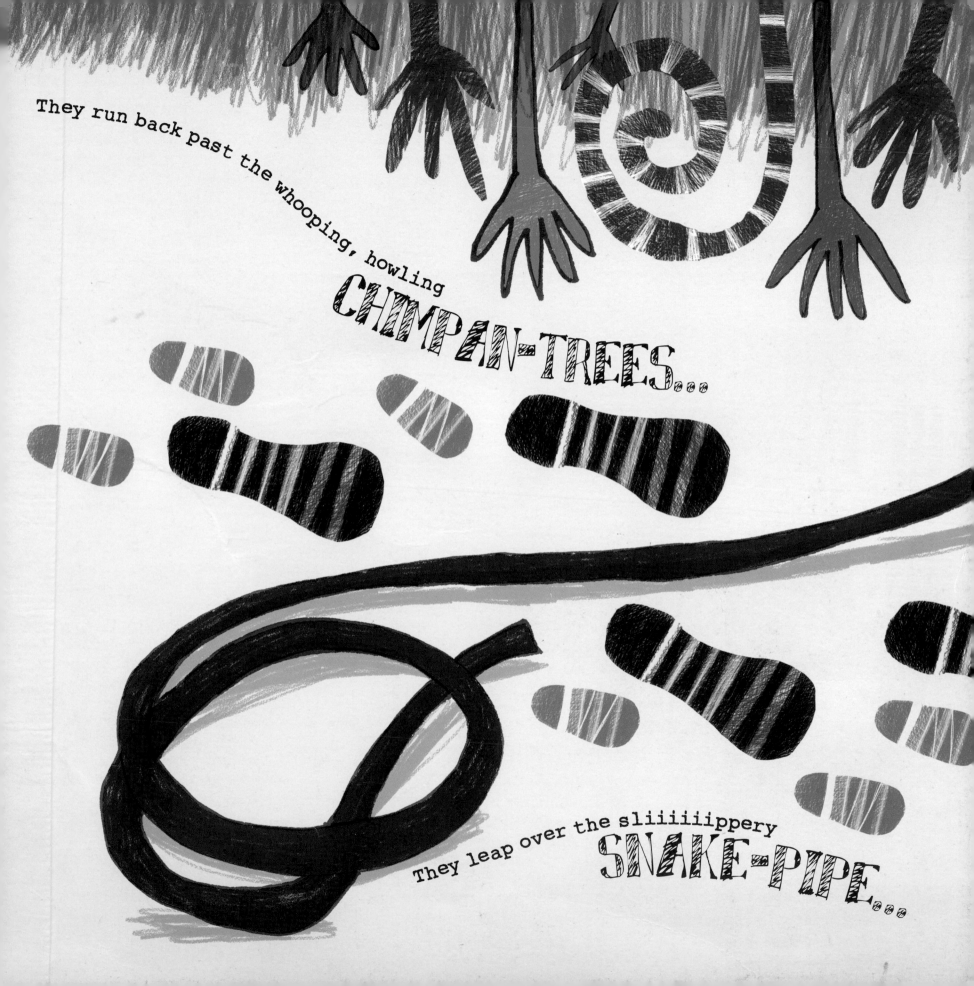

They run back past the whooping, howling **CHIMPAN-TREES...**

They leap over the sliiiiiippery **SNAKE-PIPE...**

They dodge past the heavy **HIPPO-POTTA-COMPOST...**

And they spring over the open jaws of the **CROCO-LOGUS...**

Lollipop and Grandpa reach the house just in the nick of time.

"Phew!" says Grandpa, "We were almost mincemeat then."

"Maybe we had better stick to playing indoors," says Lollipop. "It's much safer in here."